SEE HOW THEY GROW

RABBIT

photographed by
BARRIE WATTS

Lodestar Books • Dutton • New York

Newborn

I have just been born. I sleep most of the time in the nest with my brothers and sisters.

My skin is pink, and I have no fur. I cannot see or hear.

This one is me.

My mother lies on
top of us to keep
us warm.

7

Where is my nest?

I am one week old, and
my fur is beginning to
grow. It is soft
and white.

Oh no! My brother and
I have rolled out of
the nest.

What shall we do?

Here comes my
mother. She will
help us back into
the nest.

Looking around

I am two weeks old.
My fur is long and
thick. At last I can
see and hear.

I know the smell
of grass, and
now I can
see it too.

There are many
new sounds. My
sister feels afraid.

She is going
back to the
nest.

11

Out and about

I am three weeks old.
I like to leave the nest
and explore, but I do
not go very far.

Exploring makes my fur messy. I must clean myself.

I crawl along with my tummy close to the ground.

Time together

I am now four weeks old. I am
growing bigger and stronger.
My ears are growing
longer too.

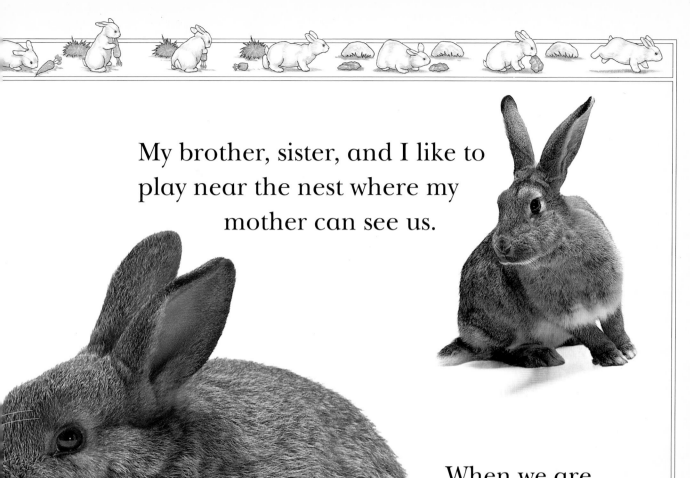

My brother, sister, and I like to play near the nest where my mother can see us.

When we are tired, we snuggle close together.

Exploring

I am five weeks old.
My legs are getting
stronger.

I like playing hide
and seek in this
dark pipe.

16

What shall I
play next?

When I stand on
tiptoes, I am as
tall as this stone.

Getting bigger

I am six weeks old,
and now I can explore
on my own.

I can dig into the
soft earth and make
myself a burrow.

My favorite food is lettuce.
I enjoy eating the crisp
green leaves.

Next to my mother,
I am still very small.

See how I grew

Newborn

One week old

Two weeks old

Three weeks old

Four weeks old

Five weeks old

Six weeks old